The Second Battle of Mag Tuired

Translated by

Elizabeth A. Gray

Published by Left of Brain Books

Copyright © 2023 Left of Brain Books

ISBN 978-1-397-66702-1

First Edition

PUBLISHER'S PREFACE

About the Book

"Cath Maige Tuireadh (the (second) Battle of Magh Tuiredh) is a tale of the Irish Mythological Cycle in which the Tuatha Dé Danann defeat their enemies, the Fomorians. It expands on references to the battle in Lebor Gabála Érenn and the Irish Annals, and is one of the richest sources of tales of the former Irish gods. It is found in a 16th century manuscript, but the text is believed to date from the 11th century.

In the build-up to the battle it tells how Nuada lost the kingship of the Tuatha Dé after losing an arm and having it replaced with a silver one by Dian Cecht, and regained it after his real arm of flesh was repaired for him by Miach son of Dian Cecht. For his efforts Miach was killed by his father out of jealousy. It also tells of the half-Fomorian Bres, who replaced Nuada as king, his conception (when his mother Ériu was visited by the Fomorian prince Elatha on a silver boat), his oppression of the Tuatha Dé, how he was deposed after being satirised for a lack of hospitality, and how he gathered the Fomorians under Balor to help him take back the throne by force, against the will of Elatha."

(Quote from wikipedia.org)

CONTENTS

THIS TALE BELOW IS THE BATTLE OF MAG TUIRED AND THE BIRTH OF BRES SON OF ELATHA AND HIS REIGN

1. The Tuatha De Danann were in the northern islands of the world, studying occult lore and sorcery, druidic arts and witchcraft and magical skill, until they surpassed the sages of the pagan arts.

2. They studied occult lore and secret knowledge and diabolic arts in four cities: Falias, Gorias, Murias, and Findias.

3. From Falias was brought the Stone of Fal which was located in Tara. It used to cry out beneath every king that would take Ireland.

4. From Gorias was brought the spear which Lug had. No battle was ever sustained against it, or against the man who held it in his hand.

5. From Findias was brought the sword of Nuadu. No one ever escaped from it once it was drawn from its deadly sheath, and no one could resist it.

6. From Murias was brought the Dagda's cauldron. No company ever went away from it unsatisfied.

7. There were four wizards in those four cities. Morfesa was in Falias; Esras was in Gorias; Uiscias was in Findias; Semias was in Murias. Those are the four poets from whom the Tuatha De learned occult lore and secret knowledge.

8. The Tuatha De then made an alliance with the Fomoire, and Balor the grandson of Net gave his daughter Ethne to Cian the son of Dian Cecht. And she bore the glorious child, Lug.

9. The Tuatha De came with a great fleet to Ireland to take it by force from the Fir Bolg. Upon reaching the territory of Corcu Belgatan (which is Conmaicne Mara today), they at once burned their boats so that they would not think of fleeing to them. The smoke and the mist which came from the ships filled the land and the air which was near them. For that reason it has been thought that they arrived in clouds of mist.

10. The battle of Mag Tuired was fought between them and the Fir Bolg. The Fir Bolg were defeated, and 100,000 of them were killed including the king, Eochaid mac Eire.

11. Nuadu's hand was cut off in that battle--Sreng mac Sengainn struck it from him. So with Credne the brazier helping him, Dian Cecht the physician put on him a silver hand that moved as well as any other hand.

12. Now the Tuatha De Danann lost many men in the battle, including Edleo mac Allai, and Ernmas, and Fiacha, and Tuirill Bicreo.

13. Then those of the Fir Bolg who escaped from the battle fled to the Fomoire, and they settled in Arran and in Islay and in Man and in Rathlin.

14. There was contention regarding the sovereignty of the men of Ireland between the Tuatha De and their wives, since Nuadu was not eligible for kingship after his hand had been cut off. They said that it would be appropriate for them to give the kingship to Bres the son of Elatha, to their own adopted son,

and that giving him the kingship would knit the Fomorians' alliance with them, since his father Elatha mac Delbaith was king of the Fomoire.

15. Now the conception of Bres came about in this way.

16. One day one of their women, Eriu the daughter of Delbaeth, was looking at the sea and the land from the house of Maeth Sceni; and she saw the sea as perfectly calm as if it were a level board. After that, while she was there, she saw something: a vessel of silver appeared to her on the sea. Its size seemed great to her, but its shape did not appear clearly to her; and the current of the sea carried it to the land.

Then she saw that it was a man of fairest appearance. He had golden-yellow hair down to his shoulders, and a cloak with bands of gold thread around it. His shirt had embroidery of gold thread. On his breast was a brooch of gold with the lustre of a precious stone in it. Two shining silver spears and in them two smooth riveted shafts of bronze. Five circlets of gold around his neck. A gold-hilted sword with inlayings of silver and studs of gold.

17. The man said to her, "Shall I have an hour of lovemaking with you?"

"I certainly have not made a tryst with you," she said.

"Come without the trysting!" said he.

18. Then they stretched themselves out together. The woman wept when the man got up again.

"Why are you crying?" he asked.

"I have two things that I should lament," said the woman, "separating from you, however we have met. The young men of the Tuatha De Danann have been entreating me in vain--and you possess me as you do."

19. "Your anxiety about those two things will be removed," he said. He drew his gold ring from his middle finger and put it into her hand, and told her that she should not part with it, either by sale or by gift, except to someone whose finger it would fit.

20. "Another matter troubles me," said the woman, "that I do not know who has come to me."

21. "You will not remain ignorant of that," he said. "Elatha mac Delbaith, king of the Fomoire, has come to you. You will bear a son as a result of our meeting, and let no name be given to him but Eochu Bres (that is, Eochu the Beautiful), because every beautiful thing that is seen in Ireland--both plain and fortress, ale and candle, woman and man and horse--will be judged in relation to that boy, so that people will then say of it, 'It is a Bres.'"

22. Then the man went back again, and the woman returned to her home, and the famous conception was given to her.

23. Then she gave birth to the boy, and the name Eochu Bres was given to him as Elatha had said. A week after the woman's lying-in was completed, the boy had two weeks' growth; and he maintained that increase for seven years, until he had reached the growth of fourteen years.

24. As a result of that contention which took place among the Tuatha De, the sovereignty of Ireland was given to that youth; and he gave seven guarantors from the warriors of Ireland (his

maternal kinsmen) for his restitution of the sovereignty if his own misdeeds should give cause. Then his mother gave him land, and he had a fortress built on the land, Dun mBrese. And it was the Dagda who built that fortress.

25. But after Bres had assumed the sovereignty, three Fomorian kings (Indech mac De Domnann, Elatha mac Delbaith, and Tethra) imposed their tribute upon Ireland-and there was not a smoke from a house in Ireland which was not under their tribute. In addition, the warriors of Ireland were reduced to serving him: Ogma beneath a bundle of firewood and the Dagda as a rampart-builder, and he constructed the earthwork around Bres's fort.

26. Now the Dagda was unhappy at the work, and in the house he used to meet an idle blind man named Cridenbel, whose mouth grew out of his chest. Cridenbel considered his own meal small and the Dagda's large, so he said, "Dagda, for the sake of your honor let the three best bits of your serving be given to me!" and the Dagda used to give them to him every night. But the satirist's bits were large: each bit was the size of a good pig. Furthermore those three bits were a third of the Dagda's serving. The Dagda's appearance was the worse for that.

27. Then one day the Dagda was in the trench and he saw the Mac Oc corning toward him.

"Greetings to you, Dagda!" said the Mac Oc.

"And to you," said the Dagda.

"What makes you look so bad?" he asked.

"I have good cause," he said. "Every night Cridenbel the satirist demands from me the three best bits of my serving."

28. "I have advice for you," said the Mac Oc. He puts his hand into his purse, and takes from it three coins of gold, and gives them to him.

29. "Put," he said, "these three gold coins into the three bits for Cridenbel in the evening. Then these will be the best on your dish, and the gold will stick in his belly so that he will die of it; and Bres's judgement afterwards will not be right. Men will say to the king, 'The Dagda has killed Cridenbel with a deadly herb which he gave him.' Then the king will order you to be killed, and you will say to him, 'What you say, king of the warriors of the Feni, is not a prince's truth. For he kept importuning me since I began my work, saying to me, "Give me the three best bits of your serving, Dagda. My housekeeping is bad tonight." Indeed, I would have died from that, had not the three gold coins which I found today helped me. I put them into my serving. Then I gave it to Cridenbel, because the gold was the best thing that was before me. So the gold is now in Cridenbel, and he died of it.'"

"It is clear," said the king. "Let the satirist's stomach be cut out to see whether the gold will be found in it. If it is not found, you will die. If it is found, however, you will live."

30. Then they cut out the satirist's stomach to find the three gold coins in his belly, and the Dagda was saved.

31. Then the Dagda went to his work the next morning, and the Mac Oc came to him and said, "Soon you will finish your work, but do not seek payment until the cattle of Ireland are brought to you. Choose from among them the dark, black-maned, trained, spirited heifer.

32. Then the Dagda brought his work to an end, and Bres asked him what he would take as wages for his labour. The Dagda answered, "I require that you gather the cattle of Ireland in one place." The king did that as he asked, and he chose the heifer from among them as the Mac Oc had told him. That seemed foolish to Bres. He had thought that he would have chosen something more.

33. Now Nuadu was being treated, and Dian Cecht put a silver hand on him which had the movement of any other hand. But his son Miach did not like that. He went to the hand and said "joint to joint of it, and sinew to sinew"; and he healed it in nine days and nights. The first three days he carried it against his side, and it became covered with skin. The second three days he carried it against his chest. The third three days he would cast white wisps of black bulrushes after they had been blackened in a fire.

34. Dian Cecht did not like that cure. He hurled a sword at the crown of his son's head and cut his skin to the flesh. The young man healed it by means of his skill. He struck him again and cut his flesh until he reached the bone. The young man healed it by the same means. He struck the third blow and reached the membrane of his brain. The young man healed this too by the same means. Then he struck the fourth blow and cut out the brain, so that Miach died; and Dian Cecht said that no physician could heal him of that blow.

35. After that, Miach was buried by Dian Cecht, and three hundred and sixty-five herbs grew through the grave, corresponding to the number of his joints and sinews. Then Airmed spread her cloak and uprooted those herbs according to their properties. Dian Cecht came to her and mixed the herbs, so that

no one knows their proper healing qualities unless the Holy Spirit taught them afterwards. And Dian Cecht said, "Though Miach no longer lives, Airmed shall remain."

36. At that time, Bres held the sovereignty as it had been granted to him. There was great murmuring against him among his maternal kinsmen the Tuatha De, for their knives were not greased by him. However frequently they might come, their breaths did not smell of ale; and they did not see their poets nor their bards nor their satirists nor their harpers nor their pipers nor their horn-blowers nor their jugglers nor their fools entertaining them in the household. They did not go to contests of those pre-eminent in the arts, nor did they see their warriors proving their skill at arms before the king, except for one man, Ogma the son of Lain.

37. This was the duty which he had, to bring firewood to the fortress. He would bring a bundle every day from the islands of Clew Bay. The sea would carry off two-thirds of his bundle because he was weak for lack of food. He used to bring back only one third, and he supplied the host from day to day.

38. But neither service nor payment from the tribes continued; and the treasures of the tribe were not being given by the act of the whole tribe.

39. On one occasion the poet came to the house of Bres seeking hospitality (that is, Coirpre son of Etain, the poet of the Tuatha De). he entered a narrow, black, dark little house; and there was neither fire nor furniture nor bedding in it. Three small cakes were brought to him on a little dish--and they were dry. The next day he arose, and he was not thankful. As he went across the yard he said,

"Without food quickly on a dish,

Without cow's milk on which a calf grows,
Without a man's habitation after darkness remains,
Without paying a company of storytellers--let that be Bres's condition."

"Bres's prosperity no longer exists," he said, and that was true. There was only blight on him from that hour; and that is the first satire that was made in Ireland.

40. Now after that the Tuatha De went together to talk with their adopted son Bres mac Elathan, and they asked him for their sureties. he gave them restoration of the kingship, and they did not regard him as properly qualified to rule from that time on. He asked to remain for seven years. "You will have that," the same assembly agreed, "provided that the safeguarding of every payment that has been assigned to you--including house and land, gold and silver, cattle and food --is supported by the same securities, and that we have freedom of tribute and payment until then."

"You will have what you ask," Bres said.

41. This is why they were asked for the delay: that he might gather the warriors of the sid, the Fomoire, to take possession of the Tuatha by force provided he might gain an overwhelming advantage. He was unwilling to be driven from his kingship.

42. Then he went to his mother and asked her where his family was. "I am certain about that," she said, and went onto the hill from which she had seen the silver vessel in the sea. She then went onto the shore. His mother gave him the ring which had been left with her, and he put it around his middle finger, and it fitted him. She had not given it up for anyone, either by sale or gift. Until that day, there was none of them whom it would fit.

43. Then they went forward until they reached the land of the Fomoire. They came to a great plain with many assemblies upon it, and they reached the finest of these assemblies. Inside, people sought information from them. They answered that they were of the men of Ireland. Then they were asked whether they had dogs, for at that time it was the custom, when a group of men visited another assembly, to challenge them to a friendly contest. "We have dogs," said Bres. Then the dogs raced, and those of the Tuatha De were faster than those of the Fomoire. Then they were asked whether they had horses to race. They answered, "We have," and they were faster than the horses of the Fomoire.

44. Then they were asked whether they had anyone who was good at sword-play, and no one was found among them except Bres. But when he lifted the hand with the sword, his father recognized the ring on his finger and asked who the warrior was. His mother answered on his behalf and told the king that Bres was his son. She related to him the whole story as we have recounted it.

45. His father was sad about him, and asked, "What force brought you out of the land you ruled?"

Bres answered, "Nothing brought me except my own injustice and arrogance. I deprived them of their valuables and possessions and their own food. Neither tribute nor payment was ever taken from them until now."

46. "That is bad," said his father. "Better their prosperity than their kingship. Better their requests than their curses. Why then have you come?" asked his father.

47. "I have come to ask you for warriors," he said. "I intend to take that land by force."

48. "You ought not to gain it by injustice if you do not gain it by justice," he said.

49. "I have a question then: what advice do you have for me?" said Bres.

50. After that he sent him to the champion Balor, grandson of Net, the king of the Hebrides, and to Indech mac De Domnann, the king of the Fomoire; and these gathered all the forces from Lochlainn westwards to Ireland, to impose their tribute and their rule upon them by force, and they made a single bridge of ships from the Hebrides to Ireland.

51. No host ever came to Ireland which was more terrifying or dreadful than that host of the Fomoire. There was rivalry between the men from Scythia of Lochlainn and the men out of the Hebrides concerning that expedition.

52. As for the Tuatha De, however, that is discussed here.

53. After Bres, Nuadu was once more in the kingship over the Tuatha De; and at that time he held a great feast for the Tuatha De in Tara. Now there was a certain warrior whose name was Samildanach on his way to Tara. At that time there were doorkeepers at Tara named Gamal mac Figail and Camall mac Riagail. While the latter was on duty, he saw the strange company coming toward him. A handsome, well-built young warrior with a king's diadem was at the front of the band.

54. They told the doorkeeper to announce their arrival in Tara. The doorkeeper asked, "Who is there?"

55. "Lug Lormansclech is here, the son of Cian son of Dian Cecht and of Ethne daughter of Balor. He is the foster son of Tailtiu, the daughter of Magmor, the king of Spain, and of Eochaid Garb mac Duach."

56. The doorkeeper then asked of Samildanach, "What art do you practice? For no one without an art enters Tara."

57. "Question me," he said. "I am a builder."

The doorkeeper answered, "We do not need you. We have a builder already, Luchta mac Luachada."

58. He said, "Question me, doorkeeper: I am a smith."

The doorkeeper answered him, "We have a smith already, Colum Cualeinech of the three new techniques."

59. He said, "Question me: I am a champion."

The doorkeeper answered, "We do not need you. We have a champion already, Ogma mac Ethlend."

60. He said again, "Question me." "I am a harper," he said.

"We do not need you. We have a harper already, Abcan mac Bicelmois, whom the men of the three gods chose in the sid-mounds."

61. He said, "Question me: I am a warrior."

The doorkeeper answered, "We do not need you. We have a warrior already, Bresal Etarlam mac Echdach Baethlaim."

62. Then he said, "Question me, doorkeeper. I am a poet and a historian."

"We do not need you. We already have a poet and historian, En mac Ethamain."

63. He said, "Question me. I am a sorcerer."

"We do not need you. We have sorcerers already. Our druids and our people of power are numerous."

64. He said, "Question me. I am a physician."

"We do not need you. We have Dian Cecht as a physician."

65. "Question me," he said. "I am a cupbearer."

"We do not need you. We have cupbearers already: Delt and Drucht and Daithe, Tae and Talom and Trog, Gle and Glan and Glesse."

66. He said, "Question me: I am a good brazier."

"We do not need you. We have a brazier already, Credne Cerd."

67. He said, "Ask the king whether he has one man who possesses all these arts: if he has I will not be able to enter Tara."

68. Then the doorkeeper went into the royal hall and told everything to the king. "A warrior has come before the court," he said, "named Samildanach; and all the arts which help your people, he practices them all, so that he is the man of each and every art."

69. Then he said that they should bring him the fidchell-boards of Tara, and he won all the stakes, so that he made the cro of Lug. (But if fidchell was invented at the time of the Trojan war, it had not reached Ireland yet, for the battle of Mag Tuired and the destruction of Troy occurred at the same time.)

70. Then that was related to Nuadu. "Let him into the court," said Nuadu, "for a man like that has never before come into this fortress."

71. Then the doorkeeper let him past, and he went into the fortress, and he sat in the seat of the sage, because he was a sage in every art.

72. Then Ogma threw the flagstone, which required fourscore yoke of oxen to move it, through the side of the hall so that it lay outside against Tara. That was to challenge Lug, who tossed the stone back so that it lay in the centre of the royal hall; and he threw the piece which it had carried away back into the side of the royal hall so that it was whole again.

73. "Let a harp be played for us," said the hosts. Then the warrior played sleep music for the hosts and for the king on the first night, putting them to sleep from that hour to the same time the next day. He played sorrowful music so that they were crying and lamenting. He played joyful music so that they were merry and rejoicing.

74. Then Nuadu, when he had seen the warrior's many powers, considered whether he could release them from the bondage they suffered at the hands of the Fomoire. So they held a council concerning the warrior, and the decision which Nuadu reached was to exchange seats with the warrior. So Samilda-

nach went to the king's seat, and the king arose before him until thirteen days had passed.

75. The next day he and the two brothers, Dagda and Ogma, conversed together on Grellach Dollaid; and his two kinsmen Goibniu and Dian Cecht were summoned to them.

76. They spent a full year in that secret conference, so that Grellach Dollaid is called the Amrun of the Men of the Goddess.

77. Then the druids of Ireland were summoned to them, together with their physicians and their charioteers and their smiths and their wealthy landowners and their lawyers. They conversed together secretly.

78. Then he asked the sorcerer, whose name was Mathgen, what power he wielded. He answered that he would shake the mountains of Ireland beneath the Fomoire so that their summits would fall to the ground. And it would seem to them that the twelve chief mountains of the land of Ireland would be fighting on behalf of the Tuatha De Danann: Slieve League, and Denda Ulad, and the Mourne Mountains, and Bri Erigi and Slieve Bloom and Slieve Snaght, Slemish and Blaisliab and Nephin Mountain and Sliab Maccu Belgodon and the Curlieu hills and Croagh Patrick.

79. Then he asked the cupbearer what power he wielded. He answered that he would bring the twelve chief lochs of Ireland into the presence of the Fomoire and they would not find water in them, however thirsty they were. These are the lochs: Lough Derg, Lough Luimnig, Lough Corrib, Lough Ree, Lough Mask, Strangford Lough, Belfast Lough, Lough Neagh, Lough Foyle, Lough Gara, Loughrea, Marloch. They would proceed to the twelve chief rivers of Ireland--the Bush, the Boyne, the Bann,

the Blackwater, the Lee, the Shannon, the Moy, the Sligo, the Erne, the Finn, the Liffey, the Suir--and they would all be hidden from the Fomoire so they would not find a drop in them. But drink will be provided for the men of Ireland even if they remain in battle for seven years.

80. Then Figol mac Mamois, their druid, said, "Three showers of fire will be rained upon the faces of the Fomorian host, and I will take out of them two-thirds of their courage and their skill at arms and their strength, and I will bind their urine in their own bodies and in the bodies of their horses. Every breath that the men of Ireland will exhale will increase their courage and skill at arms and strength. Even if they remain in battle for seven years, they will not be weary at all.

81. The Dagda said, "The power which you boast, I will wield it all myself."

"You are the Dagda ['the Good God']!" said everyone, and "Dagda" stuck to him from that time on.

82. Then they disbanded the council to meet that day three years later.

83. Then after the preparation for the battle had been settled, Lug and the Dagda and Ogma went to the three gods of Danu, and they gave Lug equipment for the battle; and for seven years they had been preparing for them and making their weapons.

Then she said to him, "Undertake a battle of overthrowing." The Morrigan said to Lug,

"Awake. . . ."

Then Figol mac Mamois, the druid, was prophesying the battle and strengthening the Tuatha De, saying,

"Battle will be waged.

84. The Dagda had a house in Glen Edin in the north, and he had arranged to meet a woman in Glen Edin a year from that day, near the All Hallows of the battle. The Unshin of Connacht roars to the south of it.

He saw the woman at the Unshin in Corann, washing, with one of her feet at Allod Echae (that is, Aghanagh) south of the water and the other at Lisconny north of the water. There were nine loosened tresses on her head. The Dagda spoke with her, and they united. "The Bed of the Couple" was the name of that place from that time on. (The woman mentioned here is the Morrigan.)

85. Then she told the Dagda that the Fomoire would land at Mag Ceidne, and that he should summon the aes dana of Ireland to meet her at the Ford of the Unshin, and she would go into Scetne to destroy Indech mac De Domnann, the king of the Fomoire, and would take from him the blood of his heart and the kidneys of his valor. Later she gave two handfuls of that blood to the hosts that were waiting at the Ford of the Unshin. Its name became "The Ford of Destruction" because of that destruction of the king.

86. So the aes dana did that, and they chanted spells against the Fomorian hosts.

87. This was a week before All Hallows, and they all dispersed until all the men of Ireland came together the day before All

Hallows. Their number was six times thirty hundred, that is, each third consisted of twice thirty hundred.

88. Then Lug sent the Dagda to spy on the Fomoire and to delay them until the men of Ireland came to the battle.

89. Then the Dagda went to the Fomorian camp and asked them for a truce of battle. This was granted to him as he asked. The Fomoire made porridge for him to mock him, because his love of porridge was great. They filled for him the king's cauldron, which was five fists deep, and poured four score gallons of new milk and the same quantity of meal and fat into it. They put goats and sheep and swine into it, and boiled them all together with the porridge. Then they poured it into a hole in the ground, and Indech said to him that he would be killed unless he consumed it all; he should eat his fill so that he might not satirize the Fomoire.

90. Then the Dagda took his ladle, and it was big enough for a man and a woman to lie in the middle of it. These are the bits that were in it: halves of salted swine and a quarter of lard.

91. Then the Dagda said, "This is good food if its broth is equal to its taste." But when he would put the full ladle into his mouth he said, "'Its poor bits do not spoil it,' says the wise old man."

92. Then at the end he scraped his bent finger over the bottom of the hole among mould and gravel. He fell asleep then after eating his porridge. His belly was as big as a house cauldron, and the Fomoire laughed at it.

93. Then he went away from them to Traigh Eabha. It was not easy for the warrior to move along on account of the size of his belly. His appearance was unsightly: he had a cape to the hollow of his elbows, and a gray-brown tunic around him as far as the

swelling of his rump. He trailed behind him a wheeled fork which was the work of eight men to move, and its track was enough for the boundary ditch of a province. It is called "The Track of the Dagda's Club" for that reason. His long penis was uncovered. He had on two shoes of horsehide with the hair outside.

As he went along he saw a girl in front of him, a good-looking young woman with an excellent figure, her hair in beautiful tresses. The Dagda desired her, but he was impotent on account of his belly. The girl began to mock him, then she began wrestling with him. She hurled him so that he sank to the hollow of his rump in the ground. He looked at her angrily and asked, "What business did you have, girl, heaving me out of my right way?"

"This business: to get you to carry me on your back to my father's house."

"Who is your father?" he asked.

"I am the daughter of Indech, son of De Domnann," she said.

She fell upon him again and beat him hard, so that the furrow around him filled with the excrement from his belly; and she satirized him three times so that he would carry her upon his back.

He said that it was a ges for him to carry anyone who would not call him by his name.

"What is your name?" she asked.

"Fer Benn," he said.

"That name is too much!" she said. "Get up, carry me on your back, Fer Benn."

"That is indeed not my name," he said.

"What is?" she asked.

"Fer Benn Mach," he answered.

"Get up, carry me on your back, Fer Benn Mach," she said.

"That is not my name," he said.

"What is?" she asked. Then he told her the whole thing. She replied immediately and said, "Get up, carry me on your back, Fer Benn Bruach Brogaill Broumide Cerbad Caic Rolaig Builc Labair Cerrce Di Brig Oldathair Boith Athgen mBethai Brightere Tri Carboid Roth Rimaire Riog Scotbe Obthe Olaithbe. . . . Get up, carry me away from here!"

"Do not mock me any more, girl," he said.

"It will certainly be hard," she said.

Then he moved out of the hole, after letting go the contents of his belly, and the girl had waited for that for a long time. He got up then, and took the girl on his back; and he put three stones in his belt. Each stone fell from it in turn-and it has been said that they were his testicles which fell from it. The girl jumped on him and struck him across the rump, and her curly pubic hair was revealed. Then the Dagda gained a mistress, and they made love. The mark remains at Beltraw Strand where they came together.

Then the girl said to him, "You will not go to the battle by any means."

"Certainly I will go," said the Dagda.

"You will not go," said the woman, "because I will be a stone at the mouth of every ford you will cross."

"That will be true," said the Dagda, "but you will not keep me from it. I will tread heavily on every stone, and the trace of my heel will remain on every stone forever."

"That will be true, but they will be turned over so that you may not see them. You will not go past me until I summon the sons of Tethra from the sid-mounds, because I will be a giant oak in every ford and in every pass you will cross."

"I will indeed go past," said the Dagda, "and the mark of my axe will remain in every oak forever." (And people have remarked upon the mark of the Dagda's axe.)

Then however she said, "Allow the Fomoire to enter the land, because the men of Ireland have all come together in one place." She said that she would hinder the Fomoire, and she would sing spells against them, and she would practice the deadly art of the wand against them--and she alone would take on a ninth part of the host.

94. The Fomoire advanced until their tenths were in Scetne. The men of Ireland were in Mag Aurfolaig. At this point these two hosts were threatening battle.

"Do the men of Ireland undertake to give battle to us?" said Bres mac Elathan to Indech mac De Domnann.

"I will give the same," said Indech, "so that their bones will be small if they do not pay their tribute."

95. In order to protect him, the men of Ireland had agreed to keep Lug from the battle. His nine foster fathers came to guard him: Tollusdam and Echdam and Eru, Rechtaid Finn and Fosad and Feidlimid, Ibar and Scibar and Minn. They feared an early death for the warrior because of the great number of his arts. For that reason they did not let him go to the battle.

96. Then the men of rank among the Tuatha De were assembled around Lug. He asked his smith, Goibniu, what power he wielded for them.

97. "Not hard to say," he said. "Even if the men of Ireland continue the battle for seven years, for every spear that separates from its shaft or sword that will break in battle, I will provide a new weapon in its place. No spearpoint which my hand forges will make a missing cast. No skin which it pierces will taste life afterward. Dolb, the Fomorian smith, cannot do that. I am now concerned with my preparation for the battle of Mag Tuired."

98. "And you, Dian Cecht," said Lug, "what power do you wield?"

99. "Not hard to say," he said. "Any man who will be wounded there, unless his head is cut off, or the membrane of his brain or his spinal cord is severed, I will make him perfectly whole in the battle on the next day."

100. "And you, Credne," Lug said to his brazier, "what is your power in the battle?"

101. "Not hard to answer," said Credne. "I will supply them all with rivets for their spears and hilts for their swords and bosses and rims for their shields."

102. "And you, Luchta," Lug said to his carpenter, "what power would you attain in the battle?"

103. "Not hard to answer," said Luchta. "I will supply them all with whatever shields and spearshafts they need."

104. "And you, Ogma," said Lug to his champion, "what is your power in the battle?"

105. "Not hard to say," he said. "Being a match for the king and holding my own against twenty-seven of his friends, while winning a third of the battle for the men of Ireland."

106. "And you, Morrigan," said Lug, "what power?"

107. "Not hard to say," she said. "I have stood fast; I shall pursue what was watched; I will be able to kill; I will be able to destroy those who might be subdued."

108. "And you, sorcerers," said Lug, "what power?"

109. "Not hard to say," said the sorcerers. "Their white soles will be visible after they have been overthrown by our craft, so that they can easily be killed; and we will take two-thirds of their strength from them, and prevent them from urinating."

110. "And you, cupbearers," said Lug, "what power?"

111. "Not hard to say," said the cupbearers. "We will bring a great thirst upon them, and they will not find drink to quench it."

112. "And you, druids," said Lug, "what power?"

113. "Not hard to say," said the druids. "We will bring showers of fire upon the faces of the Fomoire so that they cannot look up, and the warriors contending with them can use their force to kill them."

114. "And you, Coirpre mac Etaine," said Lug to his poet, "what can you do in the battle?"

115. "Not hard to say," said Coirpre. "I will make a glam dicenn against them, and I will satirize them and shame them so that through the spell of my art they will offer no resistance to warriors."

116. "And you, Be Chuille and Dianann," said Lug to his two witches, "what can you do in the battle?"

117. "Not hard to say," they said. "We will enchant the trees and the stones and the sods of the earth so that they will be a host under arms against them; and they will scatter in flight terrified and trembling."

118. "And you, Dagda," said Lug, "what power can you wield against the Fomorian host in the battle?"

119. "Not hard to say," said the Dagda. "I will fight for the men of Ireland with mutual smiting and destruction and wizardry. Their bones under my club will soon be as many as hailstones under the feet of herds of horses, where the double enemy meets on the battlefield of Mag Tuired."

120. Then in this way Lug addressed each of them in turn concerning their arts, strengthening them and addressing them in such a way that every man had the courage of a king or great lord.

121. Now every day the battle was drawn up between the race of the Fomoire and the Tuatha De Danann, but there were no kings or princes waging it, only fierce and arrogant men.

122. One thing which became evident to the Fomoire in the battle seemed remarkable to them. Their weapons, their spears and their swords, were blunted; and those of their men who were killed did not come back the next day. That was not the case with the Tuatha De Danann: although their weapons were blunted one day, they were restored the next because Goibniu the smith was in the smithy making swords and spears and javelins. He would make those weapons with three strokes. Then Luchta the carpenter would make the spearshafts in three chippings, and the third chipping was a finish and would set them in the socket of the spear. After the spearheads were in the side of the forge he would throw the sockets with the shafts, and it was not necessary to set them again. Then Credne the brazier would make the rivets with three strokes, and he would throw the sockets of the spears at them, and it was not necessary to drill holes for them; and they stayed together this way.

123. Now this is what used to kindle the warriors who were wounded there so that they were more fiery the next day: Dian Cecht, his two sons Octriuil and Miach, and his daughter Airmed were chanting spells over the well named Slaine. They would cast their mortally-wounded men into it as they were struck down; and they were alive when they came out. Their mortally-

wounded were healed through the power of the incantation made by the four physicians who were around the well.

124. Now that was damaging to the Fomoire, and they picked a man to reconnoitre the battle and the practices of the Tuatha De--Ruadan, the son of Bres and of Brig, the daughter of the Dagda-because he was a son and a grandson of the Tuatha De. Then he described to the Fomoire the work of the smith and the carpenter and the brazier and the four physicians who were around the well. They sent him back to kill one of the aes dana, Goibniu. He requested a spearpoint from him, its rivets from the brazier, and its shaft from the carpenter; and everything was given to him as he asked. Now there was a woman there grinding weapons, Cron the mother of Fianlach; and she ground Ruadan's spear. So the spear was given to Ruadan by his maternal kin, and for that reason a weaver's beam is still called "the spear of the maternal kin" in Ireland.

125. But after the spear had been given to him, Ruadan turned and wounded Goibniu. He pulled out the spear and hurled it at Ruadan so that it went through him; and he died in his father's presence in the Fomorian assembly. Brig came and keened for her son. At first she shrieked, in the end she wept. Then for the first time weeping and shrieking were heard in Ireland. (Now she is the Brig who invented a whistle for signalling at night.)

126. Then Goibniu went into the well and he became whole. The Fomoire had a warrior named Ochtriallach, the son of the Fomorian king Indech mac De Domnann. He suggested that every single man they had should bring a stone from the stones of the river Drowes to cast into the well Slaine in Achad Abla to the west of Mag Tuired, to the east of Lough Arrow. They went, and every man put a stone into the well. For that reason the cairn is called Ochtriallach's Cairn. But another name for that

well is Loch Luibe, because Dian Cecht put into it every herb that grew in Ireland.

127. Now when the time came for the great battle, the Fomoire marched out of their encampment and formed themselves into strong indestructible battalions. There was not a chief nor a skilled warrior among them without armor against his skin, a helmet on his head, a broad . . . spear in his right hand, a heavy sharp sword on his belt, a strong shield on his shoulder. To attack the Fomorian host that day was "striking a head against a cliff," was "a hand in a serpent's nest," was "a face brought close to fire."

128. These were the kings and leaders who were encouraging the Fomorian host: Balor son of Dot son of Net, Bres mac Elathan, Tuire Tortbuillech mac Lobois, Goll and Irgoll, Loscen-nlomm mac Lommgluinigh, Indech mac De Domnann, king of the Fomoire, Ochtriallach mac Indich, Omna and Bagna, Elatha mac Delbaith.

129. On the other side, the Tuatha De Danann arose and left his nine companions guarding Lug, and went to join the battle. But when the battle ensued, Lug escaped from the guard set over him, as a chariot-fighter, and it was he who was in front of the battalion of the Tuatha De. Then a keen and cruel battle was fought between the race of the Fomoire and the men of Ireland.

Lug was urging the men of Ireland to fight the battle fiercely so they should not be in bondage any longer, because it was better for them to find death while protecting their fatherland than to be in bondage and under tribute as they had been. Then Lug chanted the spell which follows, going around the men of Ireland on one foot and with one eye closed. . . .

130. The hosts gave a great shout as they went into battle. Then they came together, and each of them began to strike the other.

131. Many beautiful men fell there in the stall of death. Great was the slaughter and the grave-lying which took place there. Pride and shame were there side by side. There was anger and indignation. Abundant was the stream of blood over the white skin of young warriors mangled by the hands of bold men while rushing into danger for shame. Harsh was the noise made by the multitude of warriors and champions protecting their swords and shields and bodies while others were striking them with spears and swords. Harsh too the tumult all over the battlefield-the shouting of the warriors and the clashing of bright shields, the swish of swords and ivory-hilted blades, the clatter and rattling of the quivers, the hum and whirr of spears and javelins, the crashing strokes of weapons.

132. As they hacked at each other their fingertips and their feet almost met; and because of the slipperiness of the blood under the warriors' feet, they kept failing down, and their heads were cut off them as they sat. A gory, wound-inflicting, sharp, bloody battle was upheaved, and spearshafts were reddened in the hands of foes.

133. Then Nuadu Silverhand and Macha the daughter of Ernmas fell at the hands of Balor grandson of Net. Casmael fell at the hands of Ochtriallach son of Indech. Lug and Balor of the piercing eye met in the battle. The latter had a destructive eye which was never opened except on a battlefield. Four men would raise the lid of the eye by a polished ring in its lid. The host which looked at that eye, even if they were many thousands in number, would offer no resistance to warriors. It had that poisonous power for this reason: once his father's druids were brewing magic. He came and looked over the

window, and the fumes of the concoction affected the eye and the venomous power of the brew settled in it. Then he and Lug met. . . .

134. "Lift up my eyelid, lad," said Balor, "so I may see the talkative fellow who is conversing with me."

135. The lid was raised from Balor's eye. Then Lug cast a sling stone at him which carried the eye through his head, and it was his own host that looked at it. He fell on top of the Fomorian host so that twenty-seven of them died under his side; and the crown of his head struck against the breast of Indech mac De Domnann so that a gush of blood spouted over his lips.

136. "Let Loch Lethglas ["Halfgreen"], my poet, be summoned to me," said Indech. (He was half green from the ground to the crown of his head.) He came to him. "Find out for me," said Indech, "who hurled this cast at me." . . . Then Loch Lethglas said,

"Declare, who is the man? . . ."

Then Lug said these words in answer to him,

"A man cast
Who does not fear you.

137. Then the Morrigan the daughter of Ernmas came, and she was strengthening the Tuatha De to fight the battle resolutely and fiercely. She then chanted the following poem:

"Kings arise to the battle! . . ."

138. Immediately afterwards the battle broke, and the Fomoire were driven to the sea. The champion Ogma son of Elatha and Indech mac De Domnann fell together in single combat.

139. Loch Lethglas asked Lug for quarter. "Grant my three requests," said Lug.

140. "You will have them," said Loch. "I will remove the need to guard against the Fomoire from Ireland forever; and whatever judgement your tongue will deliver in any difficult case, it will resolve the matter until the end of fife."

141. So Loch was spared. Then he chanted "The Decree of Fastening" to the Gaels. . . .

142. Then Loch said that he would give names to Lug's nine chariots because he had been spared. So Lug said that he should name them. Loch answered and said, "Luachta, Anagat, Achad, Feochair, Fer, Golla, Fosad, Craeb, Carpat."

143. "A question then: what are the names of the charioteers who were in them?"

"Medol, Medon, Moth, Mothach, Foimtinne, Tenda, Tres, Morb."

144. "What are the names of the goads which were in their hands?"

"Fes, Res, Roches, Anagar, Each, Canna, Riadha, Buaid."

145. "What are the names of the horses?"

"Can, Doriadha, Romuir, Laisad, Fer Forsaid, Sroban, Airchedal, Ruagar, Ilann, Allriadha, Rocedal."

146. "A question: what is the number of the slain?" Lug said to Loch.

"I do not know the number of peasants and rabble. As to the number of Fomorian lords and nobles and champions and over-kings, I do know: 3 + 3 x 20 + 50 x 100 men + 20 x 100 + 3 x 50 + 9 x 5 + 4 x 20 x 1000 + 8 + 8 x 20 + 7 + 4 x 20 + 6 + 4 x 20 + 5 + 8 x 20 + 2 + 40, including the grandson of Net with 90 men. That is the number of the slain of the Fomorian over-kings and high nobles who fell in the battle.

147. "But regarding the number of peasants and common people and rabble and people of every art who came in company with the great host--for every warrior and every high noble and every overking of the Fomoire came to the battle with his personal followers, so that all fell there, both their free men and their unfree servants--I count only a few of the over-kings' servants. This then is the number of those I counted as I watched: 7 + 7 x 20 x 20 x 100 x 100 + 90 including Sab Uanchennach son of Coirpre Colc, the son of a servant of Indech mac De Domnann (that is, the son of a servant of the Fomorian king).

148. "As for the men who fought in pairs and the spearmen, warriors who did not reach the heart of the battle who also fell there-until the stars of heaven can be counted, and the sands of the sea, and flakes of snow, and dew on a lawn, and hailstones, and grass beneath the feet of horses, and the horses of the son of Lir in a sea storm--they will not be counted at all."

149. Immediately afterward they found an opportunity to kill Bres mac Elathan. He said, "It is better to spare me than to kill me."

150. "What then will follow from that?" said Lug.

"The cows of Ireland will always be in milk," said Bres, "if I am spared."

"I will tell that to our wise men," said Lug.

151. So Lug went to Maeltne Morbrethach and said to him, "Shall Bres be spared for giving constant milk to the cows of Ireland?"

152. "He shall not be spared," said Maeltne. "He has no power over their age or their calving, even if he controls their milk as long as they are alive."

153. Lug said to Bres, "That does not save you; you have no power over their age or their calving, even if you control their milk."

154. Bres said, "Maeltne has given bitter alarms!"

155. "Is there anything else which will save you, Bres?" said Lug.

"There is indeed. Tell your lawyer they will reap a harvest every quarter in return for sparing me."

156. Lug said to Maeltne, "Shall Bres be spared for giving the men of Ireland a harvest of grain every quarter?"

157. "This has suited us," said Maeltne. "Spring for plowing and sowing, and the beginning of summer for maturing the strength of the grain, and the beginning of autumn for the full ripeness of the grain, and for reaping it. Winter for consuming it."

158. "That does not save you," said Lug to Bres.

"Maeltne has given bitter alarms," said he.

159. "Less rescues you," said Lug.

"What?" asked Bres.

160. "How shall the men of Ireland plow? How shall they sow? How shall they reap? If you make known these things, you will be saved."

"Say to them, on Tuesday their plowing; on Tuesday their sowing seed in the field; on Tuesday their reaping."

161. So through that device Bres was released.

162. Now in that battle Ogma the champion found Orna, the sword of Tethra, king of the Fomoire. Ogma unsheathed the sword and cleaned it. Then the sword told what had been done by it, because it was the habit of swords at that time to recount the deeds that had been done by them whenever they were unsheathed. And for that reason swords are entitled to the tribute of cleaning after they have been unsheathed. Moreover spells have been kept in swords from that time on. Now the reason why demons used to speak from weapons then is that weapons used to be worshipped by men and were among the sureties of that time. Loch Lethglas chanted the following poem about that sword. . . .

163. Then Lug and the Dagda and Ogma went after the Fomoire, because they had taken the Dagda's harper, Uaithne. Eventually they reached the banqueting hall where Bres mac Elathan and Elatha mac Delbaith were. There was the harp on the wall. That

is the harp in which the Dagda had bound the melodies so that they did not make a sound until he summoned them, saying,

> "Come Daur Da Blao,
> Come Coir Cetharchair,
> Come summer, come winter,
> Mouths of harps and bags and pipes!"

(Now that harp had two names, Daur Da Blao and Coir Cetharchair.)

164. Then the harp came away from the wall, and it killed nine men and came to the Dagda; and he played for them the three things by which a harper is known: sleep music, joyful music, and sorrowful music. He played sorrowful music for them so that their tearful women wept. He played joyful music for them so that their women and boys laughed. He played sleep music for them so that the hosts slept. So the three of them escaped from them unharmed--although they wanted to kill them.

165. The Dagda brought with him the cattle taken by the Fomoire through the lowing of the heifer which had been given him for his work; because when she called her calf, a the cattle of Ireland which the Fomoire had taken as their tribute began to graze.

166. Then after the battle was won and the slaughter had been cleaned away, the Morrigan, the daughter of Ernmas, proceeded to announce the battle and the great victory which had occurred there to the royal heights of Ireland and to its sid-hosts, to its chief waters and to its rivermouths. And that is the reason Badb still relates great deeds. "Have you any news?" everyone asked her then.

> "Peace up to heaven.

Heaven down to earth.
Earth beneath heaven,
Strength in each,
A cup very full,
Full of honey;
Mead in abundance.
Summer in winter. . . .
Peace up to heaven . . ."

167. She also prophesied the end of the world, foretelling every evil that would occur then, and every disease and every vengeance; and she chanted the following poem:

"I shall not see a world
Which will be dear to me:
Summer without blossoms,
Cattle will be without milk,
Women without modesty,
Men without valor.
Conquests without a king . . .
Woods without mast.
Sea without produce. . . .
False judgements of old men.
False precedents of lawyers,
Every man a betrayer.
Every son a reaver.
The son will go to the bed of his father,
The father will go to the bed of his son.
Each his brother's brother-in-law.
He will not seek any woman outside his house. . . .
An evil time,
Son will deceive his father,
Daughter will deceive . . ."